THE
DARKEST
KNIGHT

THE DARKEST KNIGHT

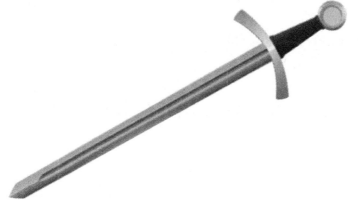

Stephen Ellis

Home Crafted Artistry & Printing
New Albany, Indiana 47150

The Darkest Knight is an imaginative work of fiction. All references to actual people, places, organizations, and events are used in a fictitious manor intended to draw the reader into the time and place of the story. Any resemblance to actual modern persons, places, organizations and events is coincidental.

ISBN-13: 978-0-9893714-7-6
ISBN-10: 0989371476

Proudly printed and bound in the United States of America.

 Home Crafted Artistry and Printing
1252 Beechwood Avenue
New Albany, IN 47150
email: HomeCraftedArtistry@yahoo.com
web: www.HomeCraftedArtistry.com

DEDICATION

I want to dedicate this book to Dr. Jeff Stevenson. He was very helpful to me when I was writing my dissertation for my Doctorate at Ashland Seminary. This small book seems like very little in return for all his help and guidance, but I hope it will show my appreciation.

INTRODUCTION

I recently completed my doctorate and found myself in need of writing something purely for fun. This book is entirely fiction. The idea came to me in a dream, and I felt compelled to write it down.

While salvation can come suddenly in a life changing experience, it also can be experienced as a process that takes a lifetime. It seems everyone experiences salvation differently. This small book is intended to show the different stages of salvation through fiction that many theologians over the ages have embraced. While the situations described may not seem to lead to salvation, it is important to realize that everything works out the way the Lord plans. We just can't always see his plan.

CONTENTS

THE
DARKEST
KNIGHT

CHAPTER 1
ODD FRIENDS

It was a day of lazy dreaming and rest. The sky was an intense blue and the sun was shining and warm. It was the end of winter, and spring had arrived with a splash of yellow, in the middle of a green pasture. Nathan lay on his back in the middle of a field of yellow wildflowers, dozing in and out.

He was in that place where you are not in deep sleep, but not completely awake either. Blissful, warm, sleepiness was his state of mind.

Nathan was a woodsman who cared for the wild things of the forest. King Randolph had appointed him to care for the wildlife and woodlands. He had the job many men craved and he was very thankful the King had appointing him to his position. He was outdoors in nature with the creatures he treasured. He was his own man and could commune with his maker when and where he chose. Life was good and he reveled in the warmth of the sun as he lay there.

He was not a young man. He was in his fifties and had lived with his wife of twenty years until they had been separated and she passed away. They had a good life together and had raised three children. It had not always been easy but, they had managed to eat well, wear good clothing, and had a roof over their head. He missed her, and as he lay there enjoying the warmth of the sunlight, his mind wandered back to better times when they were together. He remembered her dark brown hair flowing down over her shoulders and her deep brown eyes that would melt his heart whenever their eyes met. The mere touch of her hand on his, gave him pleasure. She had completely taken his heart but now she was gone. She had died from consumption.

Nathan could have been sad because of the loss of his wife. He knew life would never be the same again, and yet he was grateful to have had time with her. Yes, he would do it all over again, if he had a chance. The Lord had blessed him with her for those years and he would never regret the end of their life together. He smiled to himself as he lay there.

As the woodsman lay dozing in the middle of the pasture filled with wild yellow flowers, he thought he heard something on the edge of the meadow where it met the wood line. Much as he loved the outdoors it was still not a place to get too complacent or careless. There were creatures here that could easily do him in if he wasn't careful. He pushed up on his elbows and looked around with just his head sticking up above the flowers. This allowed him to remain hidden and still see what was going on. He slowly looked around and surveyed the region. It was a gently rolling area with the meadow completely surrounded by deep dark forests. Some thought the forest to be haunted, but he knew it to be a place of quiet life and safety. All the animals took shelter there, and lived their lives within its shaded protection. He looked all around and down the side of the hill toward the brook at the bottom of the hill that ran next to the woods. Nothing could be seen. All was quiet in this little meadow so he laid his head back down to resume enjoying his nap.

Some time passed and Nathan resumed his dreams about his lovely wife as if he was experiencing her presence there in the meadow with him. It was a wonderful dream and one that was to come to an immediate halt.

For some unexplained reason Nathan woke and slowly blinked open his eyes only to realize that something was standing directly over him blocking out the sunlight. The shock of seeing something looming over him as he awoke sent him into a panic and he tried to roll away. As he rolled, he realized that the creature was following him and he jumped to his feet to face the unexpected menace.

To his surprise he found himself facing a small pony. Not much of a menace, this little pony. It just seemed to want his attention. Nathan was greatly relieved and began to scold himself for allowing anything to get that close undetected. Yet here he was, facing this little pony that seemed lost and a bit confused.

The pony had a long mane and tail, with burs and stickers tangled in them. As Nathan examined the pony, he saw that it was in bad shape and its care had been neglected. Not only did it have a badly matted coat, it was covered with dirt and patches of mud. It appeared to have light brown hair but the exact color was not easy to determine. The poor little fellow was thin and it was obvious that it needed food and a little care. He slowly put out his hand to the little fellow who stood very still, almost as if it was in shock or exhausted. He slowly began to pat and comfort him as he examined him. He was only about seven hands high at the shoulder and he had evidence of old scars and wounds. He may have run away from an abusive owner. In any case, it was nothing that a little food, rest, and loving care couldn't fix. He decided to take the pony back to his house in the woods.

As Nathan started to walk in the direction of his home the pony slowly followed with his head down as if it were almost too much for him.

Nathan turned back to give the little fellow an encouraging pat. Instead, he was stunned at the sight of a nightmare rushing towards them!

There, charging down at them in the middle of the meadow was a huge black stallion. It was running straight at them with its head down and mouth open ready to bite. It snorted loudly as it ran at them.

Nathan could see the steel shoes on its hooves as it charged, kicking up mud from the meadow. This was a war horse and the sharp shoes on its hooves were intended to kill enemy soldiers. They could easily kill him.

The animal looked big enough that Nathan could have walked under its belly while standing — and the huge beast was coming down the meadow toward them! It screamed its rage, and flashed those terrible hooves, fully intent on doing harm. It truly was a nightmare to see, but he was fully awake and in the middle of it.

Much to his surprise, the little pony stepped between him and the oncoming stallion. It was obvious the pony was trying to protect him. The huge horse pulled up short in his charge and seemed a bit confused by the pony's actions. The stallion reared up on its hind legs and tried to reach across the pony to get at Nathan with his razor sharp hooves, but without success. Since the pony stood its ground, the black stallion tried to run around him to get at Nathan, but again, the pony stepped between them.

Again and again the stallion tried to get at Nathan only to be stopped by the pony. It became obvious that the stallion did not want to harm the pony, but neither did he want to let Nathan get too close. For some reason the stallion was trying to protect the pony and the pony was protecting Nathan.

This stallion and pony were friends – and Nathan was caught in the middle.

If Nathan were to get out of this predicament he had to take some kind of action. He couldn't outrun the huge animal, and he couldn't get close to the pony because the huge stallion had its head over the pony's back. If he tried to run away, the stallion would just run him down and trample him to death. If he tried to get the pony to move and give him cover, the black stallion would bite and rip at him.

As Nathan took stock of the situation, he remembered he was wearing his lunch sack. He had packed himself a small lunch of bread and a couple of apples. He slowly took out the bread and took a bite as the huge stallion watched. Then he reached into his sack and very slowly took out the first apple. He took a bite of the apple and allowed the smell to drift toward the horses.

The pony was first to respond. He slowly walked toward Nathan, while carefully keeping the huge black stallion on his far side, until Nathan could reach out and give him the apple.

As the pony took the apple, the black stallion snorted his rage. Screaming, it reared up again, bucked and had, what appeared to be, a temper tantrum.

Nathan decided it was time to show this big bruiser that he was in no danger. He slowly reached into his sack again and stepped from behind the pony exposing himself. He stretched out his hand to offer the apple to the stallion.

The stallion suddenly rushed him with a speed Nathan had not expected from the size of the animal. It was remarkable how fast it could move. The next thing Nathan knew, he was staring straight into the face of this huge animal – and it was not happy.

As he stood face to face with the beast, he knew there was nothing he could do. If it decided to kill him, there was no way he could stop it. Nathan was not armed in any way, and even if he had been armed, it is doubtful there were anything he could have done to stop this creature.

The animal was not looking at the apple. It stared straight at Nathan, almost as if it was trying to decide whether it should stomp him into the ground or just ignore him.

Nathan was praying for the latter. He could see in its eyes the rage it felt. The eyes were black and void of any trust for humans. He was so close he could literally see his own reflection in the animal's eyes.

It snorted at him. Great, hot breaths of air blew directly into Nathan's face. It screamed at him almost in defiance, as if he could not understand why Nathan did not run or fight.

All Nathan could do was to stand there offering the apple.

Finally the stallion decided to turn away from him. It would not accept the apple from Nathan's hand, but it no longer acted as aggressively. It was as if the stallion was disappointed in him for not resisting.

Nathan thought to himself, "Well, you think your hot stuff, you big bully," and he threw the apple at the horse.

The second he threw the apple, Nathan questioned the wisdom of such a thing. To his surprise, the horse simply ignored his act. With a loud snort and an indignant swish of his tail, he bent down and ate the apple in one huge gulp. It was almost as though the great animal considered Nathan unworthy to even be in the same place with him.

It appeared as if the conflict was over, at least for the time being.

Nathan decided to walk down the meadow toward the stream at the bottom of the hill next to the forest. He walked slowly so as not to excite the big brute.

The stream was about a bow-shot away. Once he got there he knew he would be able to hide in the thick brush and timber if he needed to protect himself. Slowly he worked his way through the meadow with the little pony following close behind. The rather

8

angry looking stallion stayed only about twenty paces away.

While occasionally snorting its displeasure and stomping its hoof, the stallion walked parallel to the pony. It kept an eye on everything Nathan did, as if it was waiting for any hostile act so it could charge in and grind Nathan into the ground.

Nathan would have normally walked the distance in a few short minutes, but this time it took nearly half an hour to cross the meadow. Slowly, carefully, he walked keeping an eye on the pony — and the stallion.

Finally the odd trio arrived at the stream. The day had begun to warm and all the tension had raised Nathans thirst. He reasoned the horses were probably thirsty too. He took his bag and filled it with water and approached the pony.

The pony stood still and just looked at him at first, but the stallion came a bit closer and watched intently to see what Nathan was doing. The pony slowly took a drink of the cool water and then sucked the bag dry. He had been thirsty! Nathan retrieved another bag of water and again the pony drained the bag. A third bag was offered, but this time the pony had no interest. Nathan thought he might try to clean him up. Slowly he poured the water over the back of the pony.

The pony gave a little start but seemed to enjoy the sensation. Nathan then took the bag and began to rub the pony's coat. Several times he returned with a bag of water to pour over the pony, until he had completely washed him and rubbed all the mud and dirt from his coat. Then he picked the burs and thistles from his mane and tail.

It was a long and tedious process, but one the pony seemed to thoroughly enjoy. It was obvious it had been a long time since he had had such attention paid to his coat. The cool water cleaned him and the rubbing soothed his muscles. This also gave Nathan time to examine the pony in greater detail — all under the watchful eye of the stallion.

The pony was a Shetland with a beautiful long mane and flowing tail. Much to Nathan's surprise, the pony was actually a golden hue. All the mud and dirt he had been covered with had hidden his true color. Now, his coat nearly gleamed in the sunlight! With a little meat on his bones, and some additional brushing, he would be strikingly beautiful. He also had a few minor wounds on his flanks that could be easily treated with a little oil to prevent any infection.

Then the thought came to Nathan that the huge black stallion might also enjoy a cool drink, maybe even a bath as the pony had. Again, he filled his bag with water, but this time he slowly approached the stallion and extended the bag.

To Nathans surprise, the stallion strolled toward him in a very nonchalant manner. Nathan thought he might be getting somewhere, but the stallion kept walking, right past him, down to the stream on his own. There he began to drink, as if he were saying, "I can take care of myself. I don't need your help."

The defiant actions of the stallion convinced Nathan to take the next step. He too, stepped into the stream and poured the water over the stallion. The stallion shuddered and looked over his shoulder at Nathan, as if to say, "Is that the best you can do"? With that the stallion lay down in the water and began thrashing about.

Nathan laughed and poured more water over him. It seemed as if the stallion's doubts about him were finally over. Then the stallion stood up and Nathan bravely began to rub his sides and flanks with his bag. He rubbed the mud and dirt from the magnificent animal until he positively gleamed in the sunlight. He hadn't thought it possible, but the huge black stallion was even more beautiful than the pony!

When Nathan rubbed the stallion, he was able to see the many scars the animal had from wounds it had suffered. They probably came from days in battle. Nathan wondered where, and with whom had it battled? Obviously the experiences had left the animal with no trust for humans. Had they hurt him badly? Was it enemies who had done this to him or the neglect of his owner? On his flanks were scars from a riders sharp spurs. The marks were deep and would never disappear.

Nathan thought to himself, "This animal has been to hell and survived. No wonder he distrusts me!"

Nathan slowly led the pony and the stallion to his cottage in the forest, nestled in a small hollow at the end of a ravine. It was a modest one room home with a thatch roof and a warm fireplace.

It was more than adequate for his needs and there was room for the horses in the attached stable. The fireplace gave warmth to the house and the stable assuring that both man and animals were warm, even on the coldest of nights.

He gave the pony and the stallion each a bucket of oats and a large pile of hay. Neither ventured far into the stable, but stood at the entrance as if they might bolt at the first sign of danger.

There was a deep water well, a place for a small garden, and protection from the elements. He drew two buckets of water for the horses, which they drank up quickly.

This place had always been to Nathan's liking because it was very difficult to find, and no one ever bothered him. He could be alone with his thoughts and his God, and now two horses.

Nathan was a Godly man who believed in his savior. It was not always popular position to defend. Many saw it as a sign of weakness, but Nathan was anything but weak. He was a physically strong person who worked in the woods protecting the King's animals, and the wood that grew there, from poachers. Nathan knew every ravine, valley, meadow and thicket.

It took great strength of character to go on when his beloved wife, Alma, passed away, but because of his faith, he was able to continue. In fact, he was known to be a fair and honest man who could be trusted. The local people held him in high esteem because they knew he would do what was right.

Because of his faith, and his practice of that faith in his everyday life, the king had taken notice of him and appointed him as woodsman to care for what was known as the Lost Forest. This forest was forty square kilometers of dense woods. It was complete with hidden ravines and dead end hollows. It was very easy to get lost or turned around in it.

The animals of the woods were varied. There were deer, wild pigs, squirrels, rabbits, quail, pheasant, partridge, geese, ducks and many kinds of wild birds. There also were dangerous predators, such as badgers, weasels, bears, wildcats, and most dangerous of all, were the packs of wolves.

Nathan had chosen to live in the midst of all of this and serve his king, accepting the appointment he offered.

Time passed, and the spring slowly changed into summer. Everything was green, and the forest was a pleasant place. It gave shade and was cool.

Nathan slowly won over both horses by caring for them, and by being very patient and gentle. The Pony needed a name, so Nathan began calling him Little Fellow. He seemed to enjoy the name and responded quickly, but when Nathan tried to give the name Boss to the black stallion, he simply ignored it. No matter how often Nathan used the name, the stallion would not respond. He knew the horse heard him and could understand that he was being called, but he simply refused to respond in any way other than to give him a disgusted look and turn away. It was going to be a very unusual summer.

One cool evening the stars were out and, as Nathan sat under a tree looking up, he began to wonder when the owners of these horses would come to claim them. He dreaded the day because he had come to enjoy having them around. They had great personalities, and were a lot of company who didn't want to argue with him about faith, politics or anything else.

Their only disagreement was who was in charge. Boss clearly felt he was in charge and was not going to give up his position to anyone. As much as Boss thought he was in charge, it was still Little Fellow who guided their daily activities. It was Little Fellow who decided when they needed a drink or food, and came to Nathan to get it. It was Little Fellow who decided when it was time to go to bed, and would walk into the stable and lie down. Boss just followed along behind. It was strange, but Nathan was realizing it was Little Fellow who had actually led Boss to safety.

Nathan's thoughts wandered. It had been the same way for Alma and him. He loved her and protected her, but it had been she who led him to real security. She led him to the Lord Jesus, and had showed him the love he needed to be saved. Now Little Fellow was leading Boss to him, much like Alma had led him to faith and salvation. She had

14

changed his life with her love. Her gentle spirit had given him a life of joy and love. Maybe that was what Boss needed too?

That night as Nathan lay on his cot in his house, he quietly drifted off to sleep and dreamed of yellow flowers in the meadow where he had met the two horses. It was a quiet evening and everything seemed good.

Suddenly, he was jerked out of a deep sleep by a loud scream and the sounds of pounding hooves! Something was wrong with Boss – and it wasn't good!

Nathan threw open the front door of his cottage only to see Boss facing a pack of wolves. Boss was standing at the entrance of the stable to prevent them from entering after Little Fellow. He was snorting and screaming his anger and rage at them, rearing up on his hind legs and flaying out with his hooves at the wolves. They were slowly pacing back and forth trying to figure out how to get past him or encircle him. If Nathan didn't hurry, it was going to be a battle to the death and Nathan wasn't sure which was going to die.

He quickly turned and grabbed a torch and a long stick he had with a nail in the end. He had used it to turn logs in the fireplace, but now it was for a very different purpose. With the torch flaming in his left hand, and the stick in the other, he ran toward the wolves.

Faced with the sight of the man and fire in his hand, they cowered for a moment, but then came after him. He took the stick with the nail in it and thrust it at the first wolf. The nail penetrated soft flesh and the wolf howled with pain. Then a second wolf tried to get at him, only to be met with a blazing torch to the side of its head. The flames burned its face and hair, and sent it running for the woods. With flames flying everywhere and a sharp stick poking them, the wolves decided it wasn't smart to stay. There was nothing there for them.

As the wolves ran away, Nathan turned to Boss and Little Fellow to see if they were alright. Boss stood in the doorway with a relieved but puzzled expression. It was obvious, he was trying to process all that had happened. This human had actually come to "HIS" rescue. It was an important turning point for both of them. It seemed as if their relationship had suddenly turned a corner. Maybe this was going to be a good summer after all?

Nathan examined Boss from top to bottom to see if he had been injured. He showed no signs of being injured, but he was obviously shaken by the encounter. Little Fellow was in the stable, a little nervous but none the worse for the experience.

That night and the next day Nathan kept a close watch on the surrounding woods, but the wolves seemed to have moved on. There was no sign of them, but for the rest of the day he kept a watchful eye on the two horses.

As evening came and the sun began to set, he noticed movement in the woods, but he could not make out what it was. At first he thought the wolves might be back, but they never showed themselves, so he decided to put the two horses in the stable and turn in for the night.

The forest had been quiet that day and the setting of the sun lulled him into a false sense of security. He was not prepared for what came next.

As he ate his evening meal, his door suddenly flew open. Behind the door stood a huge man in armor with sword drawn. This man was not your regular knight. He armor was black, and his face was completely covered by his helmet. All Nathan could see was his eyes, which seemed to glow from inside his helmet. He was the picture of a demon come to life, and his sword was poised to strike. He smelled of death. His intentions were obvious, and Nathan was in danger of losing his life.

Nathan sprang to his feet and grabbed the stick with the nail in the end. He pointed it at the knight he was facing, determined to defend himself. The man only laughed a dark and sinister laugh as he quickly swung the sword cutting the stick in two. Nathan found himself standing there with just a stub of the stick in his hand. He jumped behind the table in an effort to keep some distance between himself and the knight, but again his sword flashed and the table that separated them was instantly smashed into pieces. Nathan was cornered. There was nowhere to go. His small cottage had become a trap.

Nathan spoke saying, "What am I to you? Why do you wish me harm? I have nothing of value for you to take."

The knight in a deep, gravelly voice said, "You have stolen my horse. I have been looking for him for a long time. Now I have come to take him back."

Nathan was shocked to hear such accusations. The shock on his face must have surprised even the knight because he stopped his advance.

Nathan said, "All I have done is cared for them and healed their wounds. Why would you kill me for that? If they are yours, you are free to take them...well uh, if you can."

To that the knight laughed and sheathed his sword in its scabbard. "I see you have met my war horse. He does have a mind of his own and the smaller one is his friend. They have been together since before I came to own them. We will see if you tell the truth. Come with me."

With that, the knight turned and walked out the door signaling for Nathan to follow. The knight led them to the stable and told him to walk in first. Nathan did as he demanded and walked up to Boss. The knight seemed startled to see him walk up to the stallion without fear and gently caress his neck.

"What magic is this that you can come near my stallion without fearing for your life" asked the knight?

"Just the Magic of love" replied Nathan. "I have cared for him and tended to him since he first charged me, but Little Fellow over there, prevented him from harming me. Now, Boss is my friend."

The knight stood there as if pondering what to do. "His name is Darkness," he said at last.

The huge horse jerked up his head, acknowledging his name. It then dawned on Nathan that the horse had not acted aggressively toward the knight. He had not even snorted. Clearly he knew the knight and had no fear of him. This was the person who had ridden him before into battle. What kind of knight was he? Was he a mercenary, or a knight of principle?

Then the knight began to tell the story of Darkness. "The horse is a magnificent war horse. Enemy soldiers tremble at the sight of him, and he is deserving of their terror. He has killed more men in battle than you could imagine. His soul is as black and dark as his hair. There has never been any love in his heart, except for the smaller horse you call 'Little Fellow.' His spirit has never been broken, and only I have ever ridden him. No one has ever gotten close to him but me . . . until now."

They had ridden in many battles and killed, and killed, and killed, until the knight could no longer endure the carnage. Arms cut off, heads lopped off, bodies crushed under foot, good men impaled on spears, all of the horrible acts of war the knight and Darkness had endured together. They were as one.

"What do you call the pony?" asked Nathan.

"Nothing, he is worthless except he keeps Darkness in line. You may have him if you wish, but only if Darkness will leave without him, and I doubt that he will. If you try to resist, I will cut you down as I would any worthless weed in my way. You will take care of him and do as I say until I leave. Do you understand?"

Nathan nodded his understanding.

"Do not test me nor disappoint me, and you will live."

CHAPTER 2
NOT THE LIFE HE CHOSE

That first night with the strange knight was a time of fear and dread. Nathan returned to his cottage along with the knight who bound him and took his bed. He did all this without removing his armor. How he slept in it was beyond understanding. He clearly did not trust Nathan and did not want him to see his face.

Nathan lay on the floor, wondering what the next day would bring. He could not sleep.

As morning broke, the knight rose silently, without having made a noise throughout the night to indicate if he had ever slept. He kicked Nathan on the bottom of the foot to rouse him and told him to get up. "Fix me something to eat and hurry up."

With his feet and hands still bound, but not as tightly, Nathan shuffled around the house making breakfast. He prepared hot tea, toasted bread, honey, and some fried potatoes. The knight ate them with his back to Nathan so he would not reveal his face.

Nathan also ate, but sitting on the floor.

Suddenly, the knight rose and turned to face Nathan. All that was visible were his eyes looking through the slits in his helmet. They seemed void and without emotion, almost dead to look into. "What did you do to make Darkness accept you into his presence?" the knight asked. "No human has ever done that before, but me."

Nathan then told the whole story to the knight, just as it had occurred, starting in the meadow. He explained that Little Fellow, as he called him, had led Darkness to him and safety. For some reason, God had placed him in that meadow, at that time, for that reason. The end of it was not yet clear to anyone. He then told the Knight of his wife, and how she had led him to the Lord and His peace and safety, just as Little Fellow had led Darkness to rest and safety. God was at work in all this, but how was not yet clear. Nathan then asked the knight, "What is your story?"

The knight seemed to relax a bit, and he began to talk. "I was raised as a Noble in Scotland and had privilege and position. When I became a young man, I fell in love with a widow who was a fine lady. We married and had three sons.

"Those who knew me then do not now know my identity as the Darkest Knight." He explained, he had come to be known by this name later because of his ability as a warrior and his penchant for killing.

The knight continued, "At one point, my ambition got the best of me. Along with my brother, we plotted to overthrow Sir Alexander Livingston, the governor of Sterling Castle. When we were found out, we were all taken into captivity. My wife, my brother, and I were thrown into the dungeon. My brother died in the dungeon, but I survived. I was released several years later, only to find out that my beloved wife had also died.

"I was heartbroken and wandered aimlessly for a while, mourning her and cursing my own

22

foolishness, until King Randolph happened by and recognized me sitting by the edge of the road.

King Randolph was wise, and he knew I was a capable knight. He needed knights who would defend his kingdom, and they were in short supply. So, he encouraged me to enter into his service, and I accepted.

What the King did not know was the kind of knight I would become.

As part of my initial appointment, I was given leave to find a war horse that I could train and use in battle. I traveled the land for quite some time when I came upon a farm. There a farmer was plowing a field with a large mare. She was followed by an equally large colt that continued to bother the farmer and made it nearly impossible for him to plow a straight furrow.

I asked the farmer what he intended for the colt. The farmer said, "He is too high spirited to pull a plow and he bothers his mother to the point where she can barely pull anything. He is a hindrance to me and I would love to get rid of him, but no one wants him. He is just too hard to handle, and he won't go anywhere without his little pony friend. That means two mouths to feed and no work from either one."

"I struck a deal with the farmer and took the colt off his hands for three pieces of silver. The colt was already huge, nearly as high as a standing man, but he was to grow even larger and become something of a dream for me.

Over the next year and a half, I let no one come near the colt accept the little pony. I, and only I was allowed to feed or touch the colt as he grew and grew. I was really surprised at the stallion's size.

Then came the day I tried to ride the animal. The attempt resulted in my being thrown to the ground and the stallion standing over me. It took me nearly six months to convince the stallion to allow me on his back, but once we joined together, we truly became as one. We spent hours each day riding and grooming and learning each other's ways. The huge stallion seemed to know exactly what I was thinking and to anticipate my every move.

I returned to the king's castle where both the stallion and I were outfitted with the finest armor to protect us in battle. The heavy armor seemed to be of little concern for the huge animal. He carried it along as if it was a mere speck of dust. He truly was a magnificent animal!

Then the day came for us to be tested in battle. The eastern seashore sported several landing places where a Viking ship could easily land and raid one of the surrounding communities. There was a report of such a landing party and we were sent to investigate.

Of course, I rode the stallion. When we arrived, I found their ship but no one there. It was an easy matter to follow their tracks and catch up with them.

When they saw me coming, by myself, they began to laugh and throw insults at me, yet I kept advancing. Closer and closer I rode, until I was nearly upon them, and they realized the seriousness of their position. Any knight on such a huge horse was like facing a moving fortress.

I drew out my sword and rode into their midst swinging. These barbarians were not armored and their bodies fell like leaves before me. The stallion trampled all those who refused to move out of the way.

Death came to them that day, but it was not a glorious way of dying. Every Viking died - all twenty of them. The carnage was horrible and final. That day my war horse and I, together, became known as "the Darkest Knight."

Nathan continued to listen as the knight's story began to unfold. Again and again, they were called upon to protect the peasants of the land, and they came to their aid with the same end results. Men died. And the knight's reputation grew as people began to fear them. Many thought he was invincible and could not be killed. No armed band could stand against him, and for a while, the raids stopped altogether until a major invasion began. Barbarians from the mainland had landed in great numbers on the southeastern shores.

King Randolph called all his knights to repel the invaders. There were some thirty knights, the Darkest Knight among them.

It was an impressive sight, however, many of his fellow knights chose not to be close to him in battle. The size of his stallion, and the fact the horse seemed to be anxious to go into battle, unnerved them. His armor was no longer shiny and new. It carried many dents and scratches from previous battles, and they also feared his reputation for killing.

All the knights rode south to meet the invaders but they were not prepared for the sight that met them. There were hundreds of invaders and all armed to the hilt – with battle axes, spears, swords, shields, and bows and arrows. This was going to be a battle that would determine their future.

As the knights formed up their line against the lines of the barbarians, the shouts from the other side became nearly deafening. The roar was like the sound of a beast, clawing at the ground to get at them. These were battle hardened warriors who would not go down easily.

The Darkest Knight was dead center of the line of knights, but in the back. The barbarians could not see him clearly. Suddenly, Darkness could stand the tension no longer and reared up, bellowing. He was a commanding sight for all to see!

As he charged forward, the battle cries of the barbarians went silent. The sight of the two of them made their blood run cold. They knew of the Darkest Knight's reputation and had heard tales of him, but now to actually see him across the battlefield was a terrifying sight!

The line of knights parted to let the Darkest Knight pass through and lead the charge against the barbarians. As he charged toward the enemy lines, the rest of the knights found their courage and came charging down the hill after him, followed by three hundred foot soldiers. The barbarians were realizing it was going to be a horrible battle, but they did not run. Instead, they stood their ground and braced themselves for the impact of the attack.

The Darkest Knight led the charge and crashed into the barbarians so hard that their lines shattered before him. The other knights hit as well, and the barbarians found themselves split up into smaller groups. They tried to attack the Darkest Knight only to find the stallion's hooves, with razor sharp steel, slashing and crashing into anything that moved. It was like trying to attack a demon! No one stood a chance to bring him down.

The carnage was indescribable. Blood covered everything. There was nothing left unaffected as the swords of the knights slashed and hacked and chopped their way through human flesh. Hell was a true place, and they were in it!

The battle continued for several hours as the knights systematically cut the barbarians down. Several of the knights lost their lives that day, but the Darkest Knight lived up to his reputation. The slaughter was beyond explanation, and the Darkest Knight was in the middle of it.

After a while, the Black Knight began to see the barbarians as less than human. They seemed to him to be wild animals he could simply kill with no emotion. He was, himself, dying inside. What had made him a normal human being was dying with every stroke of his sword. He had become an unfeeling deliverer of death. No emotions, no feelings, no regrets, nothing, just the desire to kill. He was dead inside, only darkness was left in his soul. He and the stallion truly were the *Darkest* Knight.

He embraced the darkness he had become, because if he had not, he surely would have lost his mind at the horrible things he was forced to do. The human mind was never intended to see or carry out such things.

Man and beast both lost their souls that day and became one – The Darkest Knight had truly begun.

The battle was a victory for King Randolph and his army. They completely destroyed the invading army, scattering the few who were left. It was important to leave a few to escape so they could return to their homes and tell of the horrible defeat they had suffered at the hands of so few. It was the best deterrent they had against future attacks.

The Darkest Knight's reputation increased as those who escaped told of the "invincible knight" who destroyed their army. The tales grew to a point where he had become a legend. He was seen as a mystical being or some sort of evil demon, instead of as a man.

The other knights grew afraid of him. They had seen the effect he had on the barbarians, that it had turned the tide in their favor when he led the charge. Several of them had fallen in battle, but the Darkest Knight had not. As the tales reached their ears, even they began to believe them.

His legend spread and grew until the Black Knight found he had a different kind of problem.

Other warriors came. One at a time, they sought out the Darkest Knight to try and take his life, so they could become a hero for doing so.

Though his fellow knights did not believe the tales, while grateful for his participation, they had become jealous with the recognition he had received. There was no place of safety or rest for him, even among his own people.

Things became so hectic and dangerous, the Black Knight decided he must take the situation into his own hands. He resolved to consult with King Randolph with the idea of receiving some form of peaceful solution.

However, as he approached the palace, he was confronted by three other knights on horse back. All three had fought alongside him in the battle against the barbarians. They were in their armor, as if they were heading to another battle. They'd heard he was coming and were determined to stop him from seeing the king. They were afraid he would try to take King Randolph's throne.

These were not just any knights. They were battle hardened and three of the king's best knights. The one leading was named Pilatus, which means "Pike Man". He was very accomplished with a lance. He had led the foot soldiers into the battle with the barbarians and had distinguished himself as their commander. Many brave men had fallen to his lance and his sword.

The second knight was Herod. He was known as the fortress builder. He led a squad of the knights into the battle with the barbarians which resembled a wedge. It proved to be too much for the barbarians to stand against, and he helped to turn the tide of the battle in favor of the king's army.

The third night was known as Phygelus. His armor was white and not much was known of his background, but he had fought well during the battle with the barbarians. When the battle was over, he had been the first to leave the scene and return to the king's side.

Pilatus said "Turn away, Darkest Knight! We cannot allow you to pass." His horse pranced and spun in a circle as his rider lowered his lance.

The Black Knight said nothing but waited for the oncoming attack. It came quickly as Pilatus lowered his lance and charged him. These were not barbarians but fellow knights quite capable of killing him. He lowered his lance and charged as well. At the last moment before impact, he lowered himself to the opposite side of Darkness in order to make a small target. His lance shattered as it struck the oncoming knight squarely in the face plate of his helmet knocking him from his horse. There was no doubt, Pilatus was dead.

Herod also charged, but with his sword drawn. The Black Knight barely had time to draw his sword when they crashed together. The fight was intense and ended with both men falling off their horses to the ground. Then a quick thrust from the Black Knight, and Herod lay bleeding to death.

The Darkest Knight went over to him and asked, "Why?" The other knight made no response, and the Darkest Knight thrust his sword through his face shield to end his life.

Phygelus dismounted and approached him. "I do not want to fight you. Hasn't there been enough blood for today?"

The Darkest Knight responded, "There is never enough blood. If you would ever fight me, do it now or walk away forever. I would not spare you now or then."

The other knight pulled his sword from its scabbard and threw it at the Darkest Knight's feet. He then turned and walked back to his horse. Mounting, he called back, "The King will hear of this. You are now a murderer of the king's men. There will be no rest for you in this land."

The Darkest Knight rode on to the castle through the front gate. Everyone there stopped, and stared at him, as he rode up to the front door leading to the king's royal chambers. He dismounted and told Darkness to wait for him.

Darkness stamped his feet with impatience.

As the knight walked up the stairs to the front door, he was confronted by five young armed men who had their swords drawn and ready. They had no armor, but they stood in his way.

One young man, named Thomas, said "We are not your match, but we have pledged to give our lives for our king. We will not let you take his crown or his life without a fight."

The Black Knight was surprised and answered them saying "I do not want the crown, nor the king's life. It was he who gave me back my life in the first place...even though it is not to my liking. I would never harm him. I have only come to seek his advice. Let me pass or prepare to kill, or be killed!"

Just then, King Randolph himself, walked out the doors and spoke loudly, "Stand aside! This man has fought for me and this country with honor. If any has the right to seek my council, it is he."

The other knights relaxed as the Black Knight knelt before his king'. "Come inside and we will talk." said the king.

The King and the Black Knight walked inside together. They talked at length about all that had happened to him. He explained how the killing in battle had changed him and left him with no feelings. How even his own countrymen, sought to take his life out of fear and jealousy. He asked the king what he should do.

King Randolph said, "It would be best for you to leave this country for a while. Go to a peaceful place where you can rest and renew your spirit. Take time to be with your God and get to know Him again. He has not forsaken you. Go to Germany, to a town known as Ansul, but do not tell them who you are, nor what you have done. After some time passes, these events will be forgotten, and you will be able to return here to live in peace.

"If for some reason, I have need of the Darkest Knight again, I will summon you.

"We will tell everyone that you were taken prisoner by pirates and killed. That should end the myth about your being invincible!

"Go with my blessing, and when you return, you will have your family estate to retire to."

The Black Knight knelt before King Randolph. He removed his sword from its scabbard, and laid it at the king's feet. He said, "Thank you my Lord. May God grant you many years as our king."

Later, the Black Knight hid his armor and turned Darkness loose on a farm in the east to graze for the remaining years of his life. He charged the farmer with the care of Darkness and the pony and gave him silver for his efforts. He then took passage on a ship going to Germany, where he lived in the town of Ansul.

It was a small town, quiet, with many farmers going to and from their fields each day. It was a comfortable way of living, and he finally found rest. They all talked about the knight and his horse as if he was some kind of demon from Hell, without ever knowing he was in their very midst.

Time passed slowly in Germany, especially since it was not his homeland. The people were friendly, but they knew he was a foreigner, and that created a barrier between them. He sought out the advice of a clergyman to see if there were any way he could regain his sense of feeling for others.

The clergyman was an old man, but he listened intently as the knight told him his problem, without revealing who he was, nor what he had done. The clergyman was able to determine that he was a very troubled man and he advised him to face his demons and ask the Lord to guide him. "There is no place you can go to hide from God, and it is not wise to try."

The advice was timely and well thought out, so he determined that he would never kill again, unless it was to protect someone else. He waited to hear from King Randolph that it was safe for him to come home.

Time passed slowly until the day he received an urgent message from the king. The country was under attack and the Darkest Knight was needed again.

CHAPTER 3
THEY ARE HUMANS

As the day slipped by, it was as if the Knight was reliving his past. He paced back and forth in front of Nathan telling his story. It became obvious that even though he had escaped to Germany and repented, he was a tormented man who felt it better to die than to live with what he had done.

Because he did not care if he lived or died, he had been able to take chances he might not otherwise have taken. He was not afraid, because death was his ally. It seemed no one could take his life, and so he truly had become invincible.

The knight went on with his story . . .

At length, he received the letter telling him to return home, that he was needed to repel invaders. Once again, he found himself in the position of having to kill in order to protect those same countrymen who wanted him dead. There was no winning in such a situation, but he felt duty bound to King Randolph to protect his country if he could.

Though he hated to leave the peaceful, quiet countryside to head back into the war-torn country he had left behind, the next day, the knight booked passage on a ship headed back home.

The ship he boarded was a freighter full of cargo and a few passengers. The ship was named the *Sea Gull*. Her Captain was called Ahbab, which means "intelligent," and he would later live up to his name.

She was a fast ship, sea worthy, but with no outward signs of defense. She carried no cannon or armament of any kind. Her only defense was to be fast and outrun anyone intending to do her harm. Unfortunately, that would not prove to be enough.

The sun was shining as the *Sea Gull* pulled out of port and headed into the open sea. The sun reflected off the waves on the ocean to make it look as if there were diamonds sliding over the surface.

It was beautiful and a bit mesmerizing. The knight found himself being lulled by the gentle waves and the warmth of the sunlight. It was starting out to be a very pleasant trip.

After a few hours, a ship was sighted off their bow. It was a large ship, but it had gotten very close without them seeing her by hiding in the reflection of the sun. The sun had been putting on a display of light on the ocean surface and the strange ship had used it to conceal its approach.

Captain Ahbab told the passengers to go below and gave orders to the Mate to have the crew drop as much sail as possible. "We need speed to outrun this oncoming vessel."

As they tacked to the south, the other ship also changed course to come to a point of intersection. Again the captain changed his course, and the other ship mirrored his movement all while getting closer and closer. Finally, the captain decided to reverse his course and head back to port. His thought was, they might outrun the other boat if they were going the same direction.

While turning around, the other ship gained on them. Now they were close enough for the captain to make out that they were Flemish pirates. These were the most dangerous of all pirates. They were the best seamen alive – fast, competent, and quite willing to kill. They were often known to kill the passengers of ships they had taken.

The captain did not know who his passengers were, and he definitely did not know the identity of the knight. All the captain knew was that they had a very dangerous pirate ship after them and he had to outrun it.

For an hour, they managed to hold the distance between themselves and the pirate ship. Slowly, ever so slowly, they were making their way back to port and to safety. Captain Ahbab began to think they might make it without any further confrontation until he noticed a second set of sails directly in their path. It was another ship heading out to meet them. Maybe they had some arms or canons and could assist them in defending themselves. The captain kept his course straight toward the second ship.

As the third ship came more in to view, the captain realized, it too, was a pirate ship. The pirates had set a trap and he had blundered into it. No matter what direction he turned, the new ship turned to intersect it, and the ship following was gaining ground.

The race was over. All that was left was to decide whether to fight or surrender and hope for mercy. These pirates were well armed and able to inflict terrible damages if he resisted, but if he didn't they might just kill them all anyway! To fight left no chance of survival. The only option was to surrender peacefully. The captain ordered the sails rolled up and everyone on deck.

As the small cargo ship began to slow, the first pirate ship pulled alongside. Someone from her deck yelled out, "Prepare to be boarded".

Captain Ahbab apologized to the passengers, and then led them in a quick prayer. As the pirates clamored on board, the passengers and crew stood around the main mast to show that they were not resisting. They stood silently in the middle and waited to meet their fate.

The pirate captain walked on board the *Sea Gull*. He was a tall man with a flowing red beard. His face had a scar that ran from above his left eye to below his bottom lip. He wore no shirt and had only breeches on his lower half. He was bare footed and carried his sword in his hand. He was an imposing sight and seemed to enjoy intimidating the others as he looked down at them.

The only one to meet his gaze, eye to eye, was the knight. As they looked into each other's eyes the knight saw a sign of recognition on the pirate captain's face. There also was a slight smile on his lips, as if he realized that this man was not like all the others on board the ship.

"Put them all into a row boat and set them adrift!" said the pirate captain. "They are of no use to us. Since they have given us no fight we will spare them. Give them a supply of water and a bit of bread to keep them until they reach the port."

With that, the pirates began shuffling the crew and passengers toward a life boat – everyone except the knight.

How the pirates knew who he was is a mystery, but they obviously held him in high regard. No one touched him. They showed him respect, and even appeared to be a bit afraid of him, even though they obviously outnumbered him fifty to one.

Then the captain addressed the prisoners and crew as they huddled in the life boat. He said, "You do not know who you have in your presence. The Darkest Knight was among you, and if you had fought, he would most certainly have prevailed. Instead, you have been spared because he has not taken any lives today. Your lives are spared today. Tell everyone that the Red Pirate has taken him."

The Knight felt the darkness settling into his soul as he watched his fellow passenger's row away. They headed off in the direction of the distant port just over the horizon to tell everyone he had been taken by the pirates. He was truly alone now with no one he could count as a friend. Everyone there knew who he was, and it was only a matter of time before someone tried to kill him in order to "claim the honor."

These were violent men who made their living stealing and killing. They would have no problem killing him if they wanted, so, he decided, to take as many with him as possible.

As the Black Knight made up his mind to bring destruction on as many as possible, the pirate captain walked over to him and beckoned him to follow. The pirate walked down into the captain's quarters and sat down indicating that he too should find a seat.

As the knight sat down in a chair with his back to a corner, the pirate said, "What to do with you? You are a very dangerous man! Did you know that you are wanted by every Viking in the North? They have placed a huge bounty on your head. Anyone who captures or kills you will be very rich and very famous as the man who killed the *Darkest Knight*. They say your soul is darkness itself and you cannot be slain. Is that true?"

The knight answered, "Don't believe everything you hear."

The pirate said, "Maybe I should kill you and claim the reward . . . but that would be very boring. I have a better idea, let's learn to be friends. Stay with us and learn our ways, and then you will see it is better to have us as friends than as enemies. What do you say?"

The knight must have looked a bit shocked. Friends, with this wild animal? Then the idea struck him – why not? He was right, it is always better to have a friend than an enemy. But, could this man be trusted? Pirates were known to be devious, and betrayers, if circumstances called for it. Would this man really become a friend? He really had no other options, other than to fight and probably lose.

The deal was struck when the pirate said, "I will call you *Pilgrim*. Let's see what we can learn about each other! Maybe God will make us friends."

As the knight told his story, Nathan found himself being pulled deeper and deeper into his tale. It was just beginning . . .

It seems that, for the next year, the Darkest Knight lived with his pirate captors. They taught him about their code and how to live it, and what would happen to those who broke it.

It seemed strange to him that such men had rules to live by, but he found their rules to be just as noble as those he had learned at the king's table. Once you were accepted into the pirates' ranks, you were obligated to never show where their home port was located. You could never kill a fellow pirate, unless he stole from you or betrayed the code. They did not kill those who did not resist, but instead offered mercy by putting them into a boat with provisions and allowing God to decide. All pirates are brothers, but no one can be completely trusted. They also believed it is better to live to fight another day, than to die when it is not required.

These reflected a similar code to what he had practiced as a knight for King Randolph, except the king did not offer mercy. The king's men dealt in death, so there would be no future conflict with those conquered. How could these barbarians operate under the same rules? Is it possible he had been wrong all along in assessing them as less than human?

The Red Pirate's name was Namu. He was very tall, thin, muscular, and sported a long flowing red beard which he was very proud of. As the Black Knight looked closer at Namu, he realized that he was a very young man around thirty. By most standards he would be considered quite handsome, with rugged features. Even though he was young, he had seen more than most when it came to death and destruction on the high seas.

The name of his ship was *Freedom*. Namu's men were fiercely loyal, and willing to lay down their lives for him. He was held in great esteem because of his cunning and ferocity on the seas.

The knight spent many evenings with Namu in the captain's quarters discussing issues of a moral nature which helped both men come to understand one another.

One such discussion was on the time to kill. Both men agreed that it was sometimes necessary, and both agreed it was to be avoided whenever possible. The problem was knowing when to do what.

The Black Knight found it strange that they both agreed it was not desirable to kill. How had two men with such different backgrounds, upbringing, and customs, come to the same conclusion? How could this barbaric young man come up with the same conclusion the knight had come to after many difficult years of war? If this pirate was more human than the knight had originally allowed himself to believe, then he had been killing people that were just like himself and his countrymen. There was no justification for killing. The knight was a child of God, and so are they.

The knight had spent a lot of time in deep depression when contemplating his actions in war. He had imagined the barbarians as animals, fit only to be cut down. Now he was faced with the reality that they too, were humans, just like him. It pushed him even deeper into the darkness of his own guilt. He had become a murdering animal himself, and did not know how to make amends for his past actions. These very men who were caring for him, and trying so hard to understand him, were the very men he would have cut down without any thought just a few years earlier.

How could he have been so wrong? Was he wrong, or were they just trying to trick him into trusting them?

As days went by, he began to see the individuals for who they were rather than as mere animals to be killed. Namu was a fantastic leader and respected by his men, however, his father was something of a mystery. It seems his father was the king of the pirates and kept his identity hidden for the most part. He sent his son to do the work that was needed and Namu had his full support. Namu was his father's son.

The First Mate was a huge man called Stone. Stone was highly impetuous and always willing to jump right in the middle of a mess, often without getting the results he wanted. Even with all his faults, he was a person you couldn't help but like.

On one occasion, a couple of the crew members had been bickering. Stone told them to knock it off. Rather than paying attention they continued to argue and it escalated into a pushing match. Stone grabbed both men by the scruff of the neck and tossed them overboard saying, "A little bath will cool them down before they get back on board". Everyone laughed.

The ships navigator was Stone's brother. He was a grouchy fellow everyone called Drew. He was quiet and withdrawn but a very able bodied seaman, who loved fishing, and really knew his stuff. On more than one occasion, he came to the crew's rescue when supplies were low. He had a mystical ability to find fish and catch them so everyone had something to eat.

On one such fishing trip, they came to a mouth of a wide river. Drew insisted they sail the ship into the mouth and up the river where there would be good fishing. Just outside the mouth of the river was a large reef that threatened to rip their ship to pieces if Drew miscalculated even a little.

They wove through the reef and into the river with not so much as a scratch. There they found a huge number of fish and restocked their supplies. It was a great time even when they had to re-navigate those reefs with a ship heavily laden with fish.

Two other shipmates who followed Namu were called Sonny and Thunder. They were brothers, and they followed Namu's orders under the guidance of Stone. Their voices could be heard a great distance away, so, they were very helpful repeating the orders so everyone on board the ship could hear them clearly.

These two brothers were invaluable during fog. When the ship found itself in the middle of a fog bank, the two brothers would call out in loud voices and listen for the echo. If it returned with a certain sound, they knew they were far from shore, but if it came back sounding differently, they knew they were getting too close. How they developed this skill is a mystery.

They all had good points and bad points, but one of Namu's men was particularly bad. His name was Reyarteb, and he was not to be trusted. He was always flattering Namu, as well as anyone else he thought he could use. Though his motives were not clear at first, they would later become obvious. He was sneaky, and constantly hung on the edges of every conversation. Why Namu kept him around was another mystery.

Reyarteb always seemed to know more than anyone else when trouble started. That knowledge seemed to put him in the middle of everything as a witness, but never showed him to be the instigator of the trouble.

One time one of the crew members was looking for a good luck piece his father had given him. It was a shiny ball of rosin at the end of a leather string which could be worn around the neck. Someone had taken it, and he was determined to find it.

As he searched he found it in another sailor's hammock. It resulted in angry words between the two and might have escalated to injury if Stone had not intervened.

Peculiarly, the sailor whose hammock had concealed the good luck piece was also not on good terms with Reyarteb. Reyarteb was the one who pointed out the piece to the man who was searching.

While it was never proven, it was very odd that all that occurred around Reyarteb.

One day, as time was slowly passing, Namu saw three ships coming from three different directions. These were ships of the king's fleet. Each ship was heavily armored and armed for war. Try as he might to slip between the bigger ships, he couldn't get through. Each time the *Freedom* was driven back by artillery rounds that blocked her escape.

Minute by minute, the three ships tightened their hold on the *Freedom* and pushed her toward the shoreline. Landing on the shore was not an option. It was extremely jagged at the bottom with solid white granite cliffs rising hundreds of feet in the air. It became evident that they would have to surrender and hope to fight another day. There was no escape.

Namu rolled up his sails and dropped the anchor to wait for the arrival of the three ships. They jettisoned everything that might infuriate the king's men. Because it was their custom to give mercy when their prisoners didn't resist, they hoped for the same treatment by being put ashore.

When the king's men boarded their ship, they found the *Freedom's* crew all standing quietly around the main mast, waiting their fate, including the knight.

First to board her was Sir Thomas, who had been the king's body guard, pledged to protect the king, who had faced the knight on the steps of the king's palace.

Thomas quickly pulled the Black Knight from among the pirates and began to explain what was going on. The king and sent him and his best naval captain, Captain Laup, to find the Black Knight and bring him home. The kingdom was in real trouble and the knight was needed.

The Black Knight wished they would simply go and leave the pirates alone, but the captain of the ship had his own orders. He ordered Namu flogged in front of his men. He was tied to the mast and beaten until he could no longer hold himself up. Then to send a clear message, as to what happens to pirates, they tied a rope around his neck with his hands tied behind his back. Namu was given a chance to speak his last words.

Namu looked Pilgrim in the eyes and said, "I die holding nothing against you. I hope God gives you peace, my friend". Then, they slowly pulled him off his feet. He was left dangling from the mast to slowly choke to death.

The rest of the men were terrified to see their leader dispatched in such a manner and feared for their own lives. Captain Laup ordered the *Freedom* to be set on fire and the rest of the pirates be thrown overboard to swim the mile or so to shore. He wanted them to survive so they could tell other pirates to avoid this area.

The Black Knight had stopped hating the pirates during his stay with them. Now his King had sent Thomas for him, and he could not harm his fellow countrymen. All he could do was climb onto the rescue ship and watch as the pirate ship, with Namu hanging from its mast, was set on fire. His heart cried out in anguish at the loss of his friend. Namu had seemed to be his enemy at first, but the knight had come to see him as a person. He wanted revenge, but there was none to be had. And the darkness returned.

CHAPTER 4
A CHANGE IN MISSION

Nathan looked at The Black Knight and saw for the first time, genuine emotion as he described how the ship, along with Namu, was burned and sunk beneath the waves of the sea. The knight told Nathan that he hated Captain Laup for his treatment of Namu, but he also knew that Laup had only acted on orders from the king.

It would be a long sail back home, and he wasn't sure how he would be received. There were some who still wanted him dead and would pay great sums of money to have him killed.

It's funny how the Lord puts various people in our path at different times. Some we are glad to see, while others we would prefer not to have met. That's how it started out with Captain Laup. He was an older man of about fifty or sixty years. He was average in height, a little bit heavy, and wore a patch over one eye.

Laup explained that in an earlier conflict, he had lost his eye to an unknown fighter when he decided to fight over a piece of cheese. The other man wanted the cheese and so did he. A squabble broke out and he had lost his eye in the fight. His own stupidity had a strong influence on him later in life as he tried to decide whether or not it was time to fight or avoid a fight. The blindness on one side of his head made him careful and consider before entering into any particular activity that might cost him his other eye. "It seems the good Lord gave me a handicap in order to make me a better commander."

He was not a particularly handsome man, but he was very intelligent and a devoted servant to King Randolph. He had been clever enough to figure out which boat had been carrying the knight, and at the same time set a trap for Namu that succeeded, where many others had failed.

Captain Laup was also a father figure to many whom he met. They asked him his advice on how to handle prisoners and how to act in ways that would promote their kingdom. His counsel was greatly valued.

Again, the knight found himself in an unfamiliar position. Captain Laup and Sir Thomas made it their mission to make the knight feel welcome and safe. They obviously had great respect for him and his abilities as a warrior.

Over the next few weeks, as they sailed for home, Laup and Sir Thomas brought the knight up to date on what had been happening in their homeland. There had been many raids, by pirates and Vikings alike, and many people had been killed. The king's lands were beginning to succumb to the constant attacks, and it was obvious that an eventual big attack would come to destroy the kingdom. Things were in a state of turmoil.

As the knight spent the next few weeks with Captain Laup, he found himself growing fond of the man. He was soft spoken, and hesitant to fight or shed blood unless he had no other option. He also was a strong believer in God and all His mercies. How could such a man have committed such a horrible act against Namu? It just didn't make any sense, until the knight confronted Laup about his inhuman treatment of the pirate.

"King Randolph had ordered Namu's death. Namu had been a thorn in the kingdom's side for several years with his looting and destruction," the knight explained to Nathan. "Sir Thomas had confirmed, Captain Laup had done exactly what the king ordered, even though he disliked it."

Reyarteb, he found out later, in his greed, had sent word to the king that the Darkest Knight was being held by Namu. Even though his betrayal had been handsomely rewarded, Reyarteb had violated the pirate's code. When his treachery was found out, he was hung by his fellow pirates.

As Nathan listened to the knight talk about Captain Laup, it seemed as if his expression changed. He talked as if he had a genuine affection for the captain.

The knight continued to explain that Laup turned out to be a very likable man. He had been drawn toward him in spite of all that had passed. By the time they made port he and Laup were friends.

As the boat pulled up to the dock in the harbor of his homeland, Maggedo, the knight noticed that things were not as he had left them. The people looked tired and haggard. They wore tattered clothing, and they looked as if they were dirty and poor. There was fear in their dark sunken eyes. When they saw him they seemed timid, as if they couldn't trust anyone, especially someone they didn't know. He was an outsider now, whom no one remembered.

It was a truly good to be back in Maggedo after so many years, and yet it felt strange, as if he no longer belonged there. Something had changed. Maybe it was the constant war going on in this country? Perhaps it was he that had changed? The Black Knight had met the enemy and come to respect and love them, even with all their problems and oddities. But as things often go, he was to be tested again, to show him just how much things still needed to change.

He decided to rest after his long journey before calling on King Randolph, and he took a few days to eat and sleep. Once he had regained his strength, he decided to see what service he could provide the king.

It was a long walk to the castle Loculus which was surrounded by a moat and high walls. It truly was an imposing fortress, making anyone think twice about trying to attack it. Some had tried in the past, he recalled, but all had failed.

As he walked up the road to the castle Loculus, he noticed more evidence that things were not going well. The fields were not tended, and some appeared to have been burned. There were no trees close to the castle, as though they had been cut to allow for a clear killing zone outside the walls. The orchards were gone, and there were no welcoming faces as he approached.

The fields were desolate and the road empty before him. Not surprisingly, when he could make out the draw bridge, it was closed.

As he reached Loculus, he called out and asked for admittance to see King Randolph. The guard told him to go away and not bother them again, but the knight called out again and told the guard that the king had summoned him. After a long wait, the draw bridge slowly lowered allowing him inside.

As he entered, there were several guards who kept a close eye on him, even though he was not armed. They obviously did not know who he was, nor did they care to find out. He was just a stranger to them. There was no sign of any of the other knights. It was as if they were all gone or sleeping.

The castle grounds were in very poor condition. There was garbage and rubbish everywhere and the odor was very unpleasant. The people walked around as if they were drugged and were tired. Something very different was going on.

The Black Knight was taken up to the door of the king's chambers where he was told to wait. Shortly the door opened and a face he recognized stood before him. It was the king's personal body guard, Sir Thomas.

Sir Thomas opened the door and a smile spread across his face. He stepped out and embraced his fellow knight joyfully. He said "It's good to have you here. We need every knight we can get."

As they walked to the royal chambers, Sir Thomas once again filled him in on the state of the kingdom.

"The pirates and the Vikings have joined forces and have been raiding our settlements all over the country. Instead of attacking one at a time, the bands of raiders are attacking four or five places at a time in coordinated attacks that are impossible to defend. There simply are not enough knights to be in every place at once. Whenever we meet the enemy, we easily triumph, but at the same time the raiders destroy four other settlements.

Our food supplies are dwindling. Those who work the fields are fleeing from place to place to avoid the raiders. It is a dark time for the kingdom. There has been so much bloodshed that the knights have become battle hardened and numb to the feelings of anyone else. Most are even numb to their own feelings..."

Sir Thomas' eyes glazed over and became vacant, as if he was reliving the carnage of the past few years, and it appeared the darkness overcame him.

The Black Knight knew he had come back for a reason, but what was it?

As they reached King Randolph's quarters, Sir Thomas opened the door, and let the older knight enter. He then stepped out so the Black Knight could talk with King Randolph privately.

The knight knelt before his monarch and said, "My King, you called me?"

King Randolph walked briskly toward the Black Knight with his hand extended. They shook hands as old friends and looked into each other's face. The king was very glad to see his most powerful knight, and it to the knight, it was good to see his king.

The king did not look like his old self. He was thin and his hair and beard had greyed. His eyes were dark and sunken, his hands clutched nervously at his sword. He was a monarch under siege, and he knew it.

The King described what had been happening. His knights ran themselves to exhaustion confronting one raiding band after another until they were killed or simply could no longer go. They needed as many knights as they could get, and they had to be men who were willing to die, if need be, in order to stop the attacks. It had been hard to ask his knights to sacrifice themselves, but many did and had died for their country.

The attacks were getting more and more brazen all the time. It was going to take something very special to stop these marauders. "There are so many of them, and they seemed to have lost their fear of reprisal. They have been attacking at will, whenever the knights are absent."

The king needed knights who were able to fight on their own and inflict heavy losses upon the raiders. He said, "I need the Darkest Knight back and ready for battle."

The knight was faced with the position of having to decide which side he would be on. This would never have been a hard decision before he met the pirates and spent time with them. They had become friends, and he knew them to be good men, despite their chosen profession. How could he cut them down as if they meant nothing to him? Yet, how could he tell his king and his countrymen, "No"? He told the king he would do his best, but asked for time to pray in the chapel.

It was a long walk to the chapel. The knight's heart felt heavy in his chest as he pondered the dilemma he was in. As he reached the chapel, he closed the door behind him and slowly walked forward toward the altar. He knelt and began to pray for guidance. The hardened old warrior let the tears fall from his eyes and down onto the floor in front of him. It had been a long time since he had cried, but the tears would not be restrained. He didn't want to be a part of this conflict, and yet there he was, right in the middle of both opposing peoples he cared about. He asked God to help him to make a decision as to which side he should support.

As soon as he asked the question, he knew the answer. He had no choice but to support his own country and king.

He returned quickly to King Randolph and told him, "I will begin immediately to drive as many of the invaders out as possible, but I want to work alone." He didn't want to have to look over his shoulder at his own countrymen. He had been away for a while but he still distrusted them.

The king readily agreed and told him to go as fast as possible.

He was on his own.

As he walked out of the castle, the Black Knight headed down the road toward the farm where he had left his armor and Darkness. He would need both in order to bring some semblance of peace back to the land.

It was going to be a long time before he would be able to lay down his sword again, and he knew it. He continued to pray for God's wisdom and guidance in what he was about to undertake.

Late that evening, he arrived at the farmer's house who had agreed to care for Darkness and Little Fellow. The house was dark and had been ransacked. No one was there. Most likely the farmer and his family had been driven away by the raiders. The knight wondered what had happened to Darkness. He knew that no one would be able to take him and ride him. The stallion was just too high strung for that. Maybe he had died in the last couple of years while he was gone.

Just as he was about to turn and leave he heard a familiar sound. It was a snort that only Darkness could make. As he turned in the direction of the sound, he saw Darkness coming toward him at a full run with his head down. Darkness had not recognized him and was charging. He began to call to the horse but he kept coming at a full out charge. There was nothing the knight could do but stand his ground, and that might have proven to be a big mistake had the huge stallion not recognized him at the last second.

The stallion pulled up short and looked at him standing there as if he couldn't believe his eyes. Was it really his friend standing in front of him?

The Black Knight spoke and called his name again. He stretched out his hand and caressed his soft nose and let him smell his scent. Yes, it was his old friend. The huge horse suddenly resembled a young colt. He ran, bucked, and kicked as he showed his delight at seeing his old friend. They were back together.

The knight turned and noticed Darkness' little friend coming at a full gallop toward them as well. He was glad to see the pony because Darkness was easier to handle with him around. Neither animal looked any worse for the wear, but they both needed some grooming, so he set about doing just that. He searched through the dilapidated barn and found an old brush that would do the job. He brushed them both as clean as he could get them. He then gave them water and brought hay for them to eat.

Both animals appeared happy to see him and appreciative of his care. He wondered how long the farmer had been gone. It was a sure bet that neither Darkness nor his little friend would have gone with the farmer. He probably just had to leave them behind.

After caring for Darkness and the pony, he searched for his armor and found it, still under the floor boards of the barn, where he had hidden it. The helmet was covered in dust, as were the breast plate, leg irons, chain male, and his buckler. . His battle sword was still as sharp as when he had left it, but not as bright as when it was new. It did not shine as it once had. A lot of dust and time had permanently dulled the metal.

He put all the armor on, and it still fit.

After resting a day or two, he saddled Darkness and began short rides with him to see if he still remembered his training. At first the huge horse seemed reluctant but quickly regained his determination to carry the knight where ever he wanted to go. It was as if they were one in mind and spirit. They seemed to melt into one creature again.

After a day or two of getting reacquainted, the Black Knight decided it was time to begin his mission. He headed toward the small town of Goff on the east coast. He had heard that it was often ransacked by the raiders, so he decided to give them a taste of what was in store for them, if they continued.

As he neared the town, he met villagers who were fleeing. They had given up their homes because of the raiders. They were no longer safe. The knight decided that rather than attack the raiders it would be better to escort the farmers to safety before confronting the raiders.

The farmers seemed surprised to have him take such an interest in their welfare. In the past, the knights had just battled with the raiders and then left them to their own devices to survive.

The villagers were heading to the castle Loculus because they had heard the king could use as many workers as possible to grow food for the coming winter. It was also safer to be near the castle to where

60

they could flee if attacked. Winter and starvation posed as great threat as the raiders.

Suddenly, Darkness stood at alert. His body was rigid, even as he pranced to the side, and his ears were cocked forward. His nostrils were flared as he snorted the air in and out. It was a familiar warning to the knight. Someone was coming.

Four raiders appeared on the right flank as the villagers walked toward the king's castle. The four raiders did not know who *this* knight was, and unwisely decided to attack. It was the last mistake they ever made. He dispatched each one in short order.

The people cheered with joy and thanked him for his protection as they continued on toward Loculus.

The next day, when they came in sight of Loculus, he left them on their own to continue to the king's palace were they would be protected.

He turned Darkness back toward Goff.

Now, the real challenge would begin. Riding through the night, they arrived at the hill overlooking the town before dawn the next morning. It looked quiet, but as the sun came up and warmed things, the raiders began to stagger outside after a long night of revelry and drunkenness. That was what he wanted to see. He knew what to do.

All that day, he avoided being spotted by the raiders, yet kept watch on the town, while mentally noting which houses they were using.

As evening fell, he listened as they caroused and got drunk again. After several hours, everything fell silent as the raiders went to sleep.

Cautiously, the Darkest Knight rode into the town and quietly began his task. One after another he found them in a drunken sleep and silently killed each raider he found. First one house, then another, until he finally reached the last building. It was a small hut with the commander's flags posted outside the front door. He had previously watched three men go inside. All three men had drunkenly stumbled into the small hut.

He needed something different to strike terror into the hearts of *all* the raiders. He needed witnesses to go back and tell what had happened here.

He rode Darkness up to the front door and had him kick it in. He then rode the horse into the house even though he had to lay forward on the huge animal to keep from being knocked off by the rafters of the building.

The horse screamed its rage in the faces of the now fully awake raiders. It was a terrifying sight. In the pitch black of night, they were facing a screaming demon horse and the warrior, black-as-night, whom they feared beyond all others. They were terrified and cowered on the floor beneath the horse and knight.

The knight yelled, "I have spared you three only so you can go back to your leaders and tell them *I* am back. Tell them I will destroy anyone and any army who dares challenge me or this kingdom. Tell them what has happened here tonight so that it does not have to be repeated. The next time I see you, I will kill you all!"

With that, he and the stallion turned and left the house and the bewildered raiders.

The Darkest Knight could hear their confused yelling as he left. They could not believe their eyes. They had heard he was dead and gone, and yet, here he was in their midst. They began to yell for their comrades, but they were answered by silence.

As they began to search, they found the bodies of their fellow raiders and realized what had happened. The sight was terrifying. Dead men in every building. Men stabbed and hacked to death as they slept. Their blood had pooled on the floors and soaked everything. It seemed as if the devil himself had paid them a visit that horrible night!

The trio hurriedly headed back to their leaders to tell them what had happened.

The knight stayed on the hilltop and watched them run from the town as fast as they could. They headed north along the coast line and that is exactly what the knight wanted to know. He followed them at a distance so they would not see him until they came to their leader's camp.

There were well over one hundred men in the camp. It was way too big for him to attack by himself, but he had a plan.

Again, he waited until dark to strike the maximum amount of terror into the hearts of the invaders. This camp was well guarded, unlike the town of Goff, and surprising these men would not be as easy.

Riding to a nearby town, he enlisted the help of the local villagers. At first they were reluctant to help because they were afraid the invaders would retaliate against them, but after talking with them and assuring them he would not desert them, they agreed to help.

Several of the villagers carried lamp oil to the area just outside of the invaders' camp. Each fanned out and surrounded the camp, carefully pouring the oil on the ground making a complete circle around the invaders. Then they returned home to their village, as quietly as possible, to leave the Darkest Knight to do his work.

The camp was in a clearing with lots of trees around them. The grass was very dry and the forest filled with dry tinder because it was the fall of the year when everything is dry and dying.

The stage was set. He yelled his challenge to the raiders – who were caught by surprise, again! They had not known he was there, until he yelled. There was confusion in the camp as the men armed themselves and began to form into battle ranks. These were tough men who were not easily frightened.

The Darkest Knight lit the oil which began to burn and spread. It spread quickly, until there was fire completely surrounding the camp. The flames burned high and caught the grass on fire along with the forest surrounding the camp. Their tents and supplies began to burn and confusion was everywhere. Hell had come to the invaders!

The knight charged through the flames to confront the invaders, and yelled, "I have come to give you a last chance! If you ever return here again, I will come out of hell and devour you all! I will spare no one! Then, I will go for your women and children, as well! You have been warned!"

And with that, he rode back out of the ring of fire, leaving them all to wonder what kind of demon had come after them. Shortly after he left, the fire began to burn down, but not until it had caught all their tents on fire and destroyed their supplies. No man was injured, but they were left with nothing but their lives.

This first confrontation was followed by many more that all ended the same - death and terror confronted the invaders while they seemed to be helpless in the face of this new threat. To them it seemed as if hell had released all its demons upon them.

His attacks against the invaders began to take their toll. As each group confronted the knight, there were men who died, while others were scared into retreat or leaving altogether. The tide was turning in favor of the Kingdom.

On the north coastline, the Darkest Knight ran into a particularly large and strong band of raiders. There was a town called Odeggem which had large walls around it.

The town of Odeggem had been built to deter raiders from coming in that direction because it overlooked a main road to the south. That road led to the capital and Loculus Castle. The town was intended to protect the road and had a long history of successfully defending the area. There were many villages around Odeggem, and the area farmers were very good producers of grain and livestock, which were needed by the entire kingdom. Anyone who controlled it, could slowly reduce the food supply to the rest of the kingdom.

The raiders had managed not only to capture the town, but had also enslaved the local villagers. They were using it as a base to send their raiding parties out into the southern part of the Kingdom.

Something had to be done! It was a very good position for the raiders and presented a formidable obstacle for the knight.

Their leader was an old man called, "Hammer," who was a soldier of fortune. He was smart, ruthless, and he knew his trade. However, he had one major weakness – he was superstitious.

Hammer looked for "signs" before he did anything. He looked into mirrors, he read ashes and bones, but most of all he consulted a sorcerer named Citsym, whom he trusted. Most often, he would call on the man and ask him to conjure up spirits to see if they were in favor of his next venture. This would prove to be his downfall.

The knight had heard of this sorcerer and found out from the local peasants where he was housed. He lived in a wood nearby Odeggem in a thatch-roofed house. He was isolated from everyone else and seemed to like it that way. The people avoided him as they thought him to be evil and they feared what he might do. The knight thought to use this man against the old warrior.

Late that night, he made a call on Citsym. He rode up in front of his house with a torch in his hand and called for him to come out.

The sorcerer emerged mumbling mystical incantations and throwing dust into the air in an attempt to scare off whomever called him to come out. He quickly realized that his attempts to influence the stranger at his door had failed. He stood before the Darkest Knight and shook. With his voice trembling, he asked him what he wanted.

Immediately, the Darkest Knight rode up right beside him and bent down to look the terrified sorcerer in the eye, and said, "Tonight you see a vision of pure death before you. Tell Hammer, whom you serve, that I have come for him and there is nothing he can do to save himself except leave this land. It is mine and I will take vengeance on anyone who defiles it. You, I also warn. Now, go to him!"

With that, he threw the torch onto the roof of the house and the thatch quickly began to burn. He rode away into the night, leaving the poor sorcerer shaking. His belongings in flames, but he still had his life intact.

Citsym could do nothing but what he was told, and he ran all the way to the Raider camp in Odeggem. Once within the safety of the walls, the sorcerer began to wonder if what he had seen had really taken place. He was so terrified he couldn't think clearly. He decided to tell the leader of the raiders in the morning after he calmed down a bit and cleared his mind.

The next morning, after a sleepless night in which the sorcerer conjured up vision after vision of men being killed, he went to see Hammer. He said, "I was visited by a demon from hell! The demon smelled of smoke from a burning fire and his eyes could be seen deep within his black armor glowing hot and evil. I have seen vision after vision of men dying at the hands of this demon. I have even seen my own death, and yours too, if you don't leave this land! … It was truly a terrifying sight. We must all leave this place and never come back, or we will all die!"

Hammer was not convinced. He had heard such stories before and had no belief in such things, other than as omens, and this was not a good omen. Regardless, he was reluctant to give up all his gains because of an omen and the wild stories of a hermit sorcerer. His heart hardened, and he commanded his men to double the guard and to keep alert.

Nothing happened for nearly a week. The Black Knight kept his distance in order to give them time to move out, but nothing happened. The only difference was that no raiding parties were sent out. It seemed Hammer was keeping his men close, in case they were needed. The next move was up to the knight.

After waiting the week, he again had the area villagers drop a circle of oil around the walled town. When the villagers were clear, he lit the oil.

As the oil burst into flames and surrounded the town, he rode into it and yelled, "This is the last warning you will receive! You are to leave or begin dying!"

With that, he turned and left just as the flames died out. Again, he was a terrifying sight. The flames made him look even larger and blacker than he was, and the imagination of the night watchmen expanded reality. Fear spread through the camp and took a toll on the commitment of Hammer's men. They were beginning to believe they were doomed men, and their leader was not so sure either.

The daylight hours were usually quiet with people coming and going, because they believed the demon only worked at night. They were wrong again.

The Darkest Knight watched to see what the old sorcerer was doing. He had not yet left the town so the knight was waiting. After another week, he saw Citsym, slipping out of town quietly.

It was a mistake he would not have long to regret.

As the sorcerer slipped quietly into the forest, he found himself suddenly confronted by the Darkest Knight. He gave up his life quickly and quietly.

That night when it was very late, and the guards were drowsy, the knight took the body of the sorcerer and tied him to a large wooden X. He then dragged him in front of the town and propped him up so all could see. In the darkness, no one seemed to notice. The knight encircled the body with oil and set the oil on fire. As the grasses blazed away, he shouted to the raiders who were now cowering, "I will do the same to the **rest** of you, if you do not leave! This is your final chance!"

It was all they needed.

The next day, almost all of the raiders began to stream out of the town and head for their boats on the nearby beach. The knight had considered burning the boats, but had decided against it because he wanted them to have a way of leaving. As they left, he wanted to give them one last reminder not to come back. He had a surprise in store for them. In the night, he had some farmers drill holes in the hulls of most of the boats. They patched the holes with mud that would dissolve as the boats were put in the water. The boats would begin to leak and sink, but not until they got well out to sea. He left a couple boats untouched so they could get away and spread the word that no place was safe from this demon.

As most of the raiders left on their boats, the knight watched from a safe distance. He noticed however, that Hammer, had not left. Had his pride not allowed him to give up and leave? The knight wondered to himself. "Well, let him have it his way," he thought. "He has chosen to die by the sword rather than by old age."

As the days went by things returned to normal in the town, but the old leader never came out, he just sent a few of the remaining men out at a time in raiding parties. None ever returned to him. The knight was waiting and caught each one and sent them to their graves two or three at a time. Slowly the raiders were being eliminated.

After a couple of weeks had passed, the knight decided to make his final move. There could not have been more than a few men left with the old leader, so now was the time.

Under the cover of night, he managed to slip through a crack in the gate and get inside the town. It was quiet and there were no longer any guards on the walls.

As the knight quietly walked toward the headquarters building, four very big men came running out of the front door with torches to illuminate the courtyard. They had been waiting for him! It was a trap but the question was - - who was trapped?

The fight lasted for quite a time and ended with all four men dead on the ground. They fought bravely but had died just the same.

The knight pushed the door open and stepped inside to find Hammer, the old raider, quietly sitting in his chair . . . dead. He had taken his own life rather than face the demon he feared.

The Darkest Knight turned to go back outside and sensed a presence out in the dark before him. As he stepped outside into the darkness he saw many of the faces of unarmed local villagers who were looking at him.

As they faced this demon-knight they tried to assess him. They all knew that they were to avoid evil, but this strange knight had done a good thing for them by ridding them of the invaders. Then they broke into cheering and thanked him. They patted him on the back as they walked away to their homes. The town was free at last.

The knight suddenly felt tired. He had been fighting for months now and the northern part of the kingdom seemed to be quiet. He needed rest and needed it badly, so he decided to return to the farm where he had left Darkness when he had gone out of the country. It was a good place to rest and recover for a while.

It would have been nice if he could have had a longer period of rest, but there were bound to be things happening that he did not know about. He felt his greatest test was yet to come.

After several weeks of resting and planning for his next challenge, the Darkest Knight found himself confronted by Sir Phillip, one of his fellow knights.

Sir Phillip was known as an insider in the king's court and was a fierce fighter. In battle, he was an especially fearsome fighter at close quarters. Sir Phillip had been searching for the Darkest Knight and finally found him at the farm.

The Black Knight saw him riding toward the farm with determination and speed. Even a long way off but he recognized Sir Phillip by the bright yellow and blue colors he wore. It was not clear whether he was coming to do harm, or was friendly. The Darkest Knight decided to be prepared and put on his armor as quickly as possible.

Just as the Darkest Knight got his helmet on, Sir Phillip came within shouting distance and called to him, "King Randolph wants you to stop your mission and return to Castle Loculus. I am to accompany you."

The Darkest Knight slowly saddled Darkness and mounted him while Sir Phillip kept his distance. Neither man trusted the other. There was something wrong, but just what was not evident.

The ride to the king's castle was uneventful. The Darkest Knight rode in front with Sir Phillip staying well behind, keeping his distance. As they came to the castle, the drawbridge was lowered and they rode into the main court yard. The Black Knight let the reins dangle to the ground rather than tying him to a rail. The huge horse also seemed nervous about the situation. Maybe Darkness had sensed his own nervousness, but whatever it was, it was real.

Sir Phillip disappeared into the castle leaving him to find his way to the royal chambers alone. There he was greeted by King Randolph. The Black Knight once again knelt to show his allegiance to his king.

King Randolph walked toward his knight with hand extended in friendship, but it felt different this time.

The king began, "Thank you for coming. In light of your service, I am deeply sorry for what I must say. Your tactics have been so effective that you have become something of a hero to all our subjects, that is, except our knights and some of the nobility." King Randolph explained, "They complain you are too radical and too bloody to be acceptable as a knight, especially since you already killed a couple of their number...I realized they challenged you, but the fact remains the same.

"The noblemen also do not like the way the peasant farmers admire you. You actually treat them with respect and as if they matter in the overall scheme of things, unlike themselves. They disapprove of you. They want you banished and your titles taken away."

The king told him he had no choice because he needed the support of all the nobility and knights in order to maintain control. The sadness in King Randolph's eyes was real. He knew that what he was doing was not fair, but he also knew he had to do this for the good of his country. He told the knight. "You are free to go, but you are banished and should not return."

The Black Knight was stunned. He had done only what the king had ordered him to do, and now they were done with him. Rather than stand up for him, King Randolph had caved in to the pressure of the noblemen and other knights.

Such was his fate. His faithfulness to his king had cost him his land and title. He was to be set adrift with no place to call home. How could this be happening? Again he asked the king for permission to pray in the chapel. The king granted him permission.

Once again the knight found himself on his knees in the chapel asking God what he was supposed to do. He had done what he thought was best, tried to spare as many as possible, and now he was being thrown out. What was he to do?

As he left the chapel and royal chambers, he heard Darkness begin to scream. Two men had been trying to take him away, but they were not having any success, because Darkness was resisting. The Darkest Knight hurried to the courtyard and put his hand on the hilt of his sword. He gave the men a look that sent ice into their hearts and they backed away. He then quickly calmed his horse and mounted him. Together they went through the front gate as everyone stared.

No one followed him.

He headed back to the farm where he had been resting. Now that he no longer had a country he needed a quiet place to think and come up with a plan.

CHAPTER 5
THE FINAL BATTLE

The nobility had placed a reward on the Darkest Knight's head. Not only was he to be exiled, but he was a hunted man.

When some assassins had tried to disable Darkness, the huge horse and the pony had escaped into the forest. They tried to disable Darkness because he was half of the "Darkest Knight" combination. They thought if they could disable or kill the horse, the knight would be easier to kill or run out of the country.

In their hurry to escape, the two horses had wandered into the forest and become lost. They lived off the land by grazing, but in doing so they got farther and farther away from the farm where the Black Knight had been looking for them.

Meanwhile, the Black Knight had killed each of the assassins and began to look for the two horses. He knew that if he found one he would also find the other.

It was during that time of wandering that the two horses had stumbled onto Nathan. The rest has already been accounted for.

The knight looked into Nathan's eyes and saw only compassion. He had not seen such a look in a very long time.

Nathan understood why the Knight had been so quick to misjudge him and why he presented himself as he did. As a sign of his commitment he slowly reached up toward the knight's helmet and began to remove it.

The Black Knight stopped him and said, "Do not ask this of me, unless you really understand what you are doing. Once you know who I am, you cannot go back, nor will you ever be trusted in this land again. If anyone finds out you know me or have helped me, it will go badly for you. If you betray me, I will have to take your life, and I do not wish to do that." He paused. "It is your choice."

With that, Nathan removed the knight's helmet and the bond was complete. Nathan saw the Black Knight's face and knew who he was - - Sir James Stewart of the Stewarts, a much respected noble family. How had he gotten into such a mess? Good family, good name, royalty, lots of money, the best of everything, and yet here he was, without a country and nowhere to go.

Nathan reconfirmed that he would be loyal to Sir James and that now he had a place to stay where no one would find him or would know him. He was safe from those who didn't want him around to remind them of their own weaknesses. Deep in this forest, where no one ever came, he could find solace and peace for both him and his stallion.

Nathan became Sir James' constant companion. Where one went, the other could be found as well.

Sir James took his armor and placed it in the barn in the little hollow deep in the woods. No one knew he was the knight who, along with his horse, had become known as the Darkest Knight.

There was peace as the land was no longer at war. There was food and friendship, but most of all they shared their faiths and their struggles. Both men had lost their wives. Both men had found themselves outside of what is considered normal society. Both men had called on the Lord in their times of need, and had received an answer even though the missions God had given each of them were very different. One was called to a peaceful life in the woods, while the other was called to a life of war. Much like Little Fellow was the companion of Darkness, Nathan was the companion of Sir James. They were inseparable and God blessed their friendship. They brought peace to each other.

Time passed and they enjoyed living in the forest, talking about their lives and the faith they shared. It was hard to imagine two closer friends, but times would change again and test their friendship.

Once again the country would come under attack, this time it was the final push of the raiders. The Vikings and the Flemish pirates joined forces in a final effort to conquer the country. They had amassed a huge fleet of ships so they could bring a massive army to the shore line.

Without warning, there were thousands of invaders. They overran the countryside destroying one town after another. They had heard the Darkest Knight was no more, that he had died, so their fears were gone. They could fight a human being and win, but a demon was something else.

Once again, the Darkest Knight would have to decide which side to help.

The Black Knight was unseen for a long time. He stayed in the deep forest where he would not be bothered. He seldom came into contact with any one.

One day, while he was out walking in the woods, he encountered a family. He spoke with them and found they were fleeing from the new invaders. The father told him how their village had been raided by the invaders. They had killed most of the younger men who had tried to defend the village. They then and then looted and sacked it. As the invaders burned and searched for food or anything else they could use, most of the people had slipped away into the surrounding forest. Now they were trying to find a safe place where the invaders couldn't find them.

He listened intently but did not react to the news. "Maybe King Randolph will drive them out," he thought to himself. Anyway, it was none of his business now. They didn't want his help.

Over the next month, more and more, people wandered into Nathan's secluded area of the forest trying to escape the invaders, until there was a regular stream of people fleeing. They each told the same story, how the invaders were conquering one place after another, sparing no one. Though the destruction and death they left behind was unspeakable, the knight withheld himself, thinking as long as they didn't bother the forest, he should stay out of it.

One evening, not long after talking with some fleeing peasants, the knight was on the edge of the forest with Nathan when he saw King Randolph's banner being placed on a hill in the distance. As he watched, he saw all the king's army camp there and across the valley he saw the camp of the invaders. There were a huge number of warriors preparing for battle.

It was obvious that there would be a final battle between the two sides the next morning. It would be decisive and the King looked to be in real trouble. The losses on both sides would be horrible to see, but the odds were in the favor of the invaders.

What the Darkest Knight had always feared was happening. He had to decide who his allegiance would fall to. Neither side had asked for his help but he was compelled to do something. Why should he care? There wasn't anything he could do -- or was there.

Each night during his prayers, the sight of the refugees fleeing hung in Sir James' heart. It simply would not leave him alone, and on one particular night, his prayers took on a special urgency as he asked the Lord for help. He didn't want to kill any more and yet he found himself in the middle of this conflict. Why had the Lord put him in such a position?

Sir James talked with Nathan about his predicament and they prayed together. Nathan advised him that God had put him in this position for a special purpose -- to make peace if at all possible, and to fight for it, if he must.

The next morning Darkness was restless and agitated. It seemed as if the animal knew what was about to happen. He also seemed to sense that this was to be the last battle. How he knew is beyond understanding, but he knew, and so did Little Fellow. They both seemed uneasy as the morning came.

Sir James put on his black armor for a last time. As he walked toward Darkness, the horse began to prance and bellow. He knew it was time for battle and that was what he was made for. As Sir James mounted Darkness, they once again melded together to become the Darkest Knight.

Nathan called out to them, "May God show you the way to everlasting peace!" And with that they rode off. Little Fellow did not try to follow this time. He gratefully stayed with Nathan in the forest. Nathan said to Little Fellow, "Now it's just you and me. But God sometimes has different plans that we can't anticipate."

The Darkest Knight rode hard to the other side of the forest, in order to get there before the battle began. As they reached the edge of the forest, they could see that the battle lines had already been drawn.

The armies were only about fifty yards apart and were banging their shields and yelling to intimidate each other. The roar was immense and deafening. From his vantage point at the edge of the woods high up on the hill, he could see everything. It was going to be the final conflict between the two peoples.

Strangely, he really didn't care who won, he just didn't want to see good people on either side die, and yet both sides seemed determined to destroy each other. It was insanity run wild and straight into the arms of evil.

Then the clouds broke and a bright light began to shine on the Darkest Knight. Everything became clear to him. He knew exactly what to do. God had answered his prayers.

He charged toward the center of both armies as they yelled at each other. Darkness reared up and screamed a sound that pierced the hearts of everyone there. There was sudden silence as both sides realized the Darkest Knight was upon them.

There was confusion, fear, and hatred, all present at that moment. Each side thinking the knight was there to help the other side. Then he spoke so all could hear.

He said, "I will not interfere with your battle of destruction. I care not which side wins. I hope you destroy each other. I am tired of this senseless killing. To be sure this will end today, I will again become the murderous demon you have made me. Fight until you all die or, make peace. If there is peace, I will disappear, and never bother you again. Make war, and I will destroy all who survive, – and your families as well! You will all leave here in peace, as brothers, or

84

none of you will leave at all! This is my solemn vow this day."

There was silence as every man pondered what was said. Each side was stunned by the idea of dying and accomplishing nothing or making peace and accomplishing everything. All of the men turned and looked at their leaders as if to question their intentions.

The first to act was the invader's leader, Etalip. He was an old man, whose son had been killed by the very King Randolph he was facing. He was the father of Namu, who had died when he was hung aboard his ship. Etalip was fearless, but almost unknown outside his own world. Could he be expected to ever make peace with his son's killers?

He walked deliberately through his line of men half way between his army and the opposing army and stopped. He said, "I have lost my only son. That is enough to give. Let there be peace, if you will have it, or let us all die as men today. It is now up to you, Randolph. Which do you choose?"

There was silence. Then King Randolph rode through his lines and dismounted. He walked up to Etalip and shouted, "Let there be peace this day. Let us find ways to trade together, so no one goes without. I, too, have lost those close to me and do not wish to lose any more."

With that he removed his chain-mail glove and extended his hand to Etalip. As they grasped each other's arms, as fellow rulers rather than enemies, there would be peace and both armies broke into cheering.

EPILOGUE

The Darkest Knight was never seen again. There was no need for him, because there was peace in the land. It seems God had a plan all along, and many people were part of it. As we go through life, we seldom know the final result of our part in such a master plan. All we can do is trust that it will work out for the best.

Sir James returned to the forest to spend the rest of his life there with his good friend Nathan. His identity as the Black Knight/Darkest Knight was never revealed. Some say the demon is still out there waiting to come back into battle if needed.

Darkness and Little Fellow spent the rest of their lives living together in the little hollow at peace with the world. They each died quietly within two days of each other. Sir James and Nathan buried them both, and mourned their passing.

King Randolph and Etalip ruled in peace for the rest of their lives. They had both learned that war is far less desirable than peace. They had both lost so many good people they vowed never to war against each other again.

God is good, all the time!

Dr., Rev., Cpt. Stephen E. Ellis, MDI, CPCU is a retired United Methodist Elder. He and his wife live in Greenfield, Indiana. They have two daughters and three grandchildren. Steve is a graduate of Indiana University with a doctorate from Ashland Theological Seminary. He was an officer in the Army and a SCUBA instructor for over 20 years. Steve loves to fish and write books.

 ***Home Crafted Artistry & Printing*** is an independent publisher operating in the Louisville Kentucky and Southern Indiana area, focusing on works that uphold Christian values and faith, and which glorify God. Our published works include Poetry, Children's Literature, Fiction/Historical Fiction, The Miraculous Intervention*s* Series, and Photography. We will soon be adding Crafts and Cookbooks.

To inquire about publishing your book, send an email with subject line of, **"I have a book to be published"** to:
HomeCraftedArtisry@yahoo.com
(e-mail with no subject will not be opened, nor acknowledged)

These fine titles are available through
HomeCraftedArtistry.com
or at Amazon.com:

> ***The Miraculous Interventions* series**
>   by Deborah Aubrey-Peyron
> ***Christmas Chaos!*** by Deborah Aubrey-Peyron
> ***Holy Spirit Tours*** by Bob Garvey, M.Ed.
> ***His Beauty Unveiled*** by Anita K. Bube
> ***One Step Closer*** by Geri Manning
> ***Joey's Big Fish*** by Keith Fowler
> ***Echo Beach*** by Nancy Parsons
> ***A Heart for Truth*** by Joyce Cordell

HCAP books produced in conjunction with
Alpha Publishing div. of Alpha Consulting:
> ***Seasons of a Woman's Life***
>   by Carol Goodman Heizer, M.Ed.
> ***Snapshots of Life from a Writer's View***
>   by Carol Goodman Heizer, M.Ed.

Made in the USA
Monee, IL
23 December 2023

48795130R00062